To the Wonderful Reinsma Kids:
Micah, Hannah, Grace, Emma, Peter, and Rachel.

And to Arthur, whose behind-the-scenes
encouragement and insight deserve center stage.

Text and illustrations copyright © 2006 by Carmela and Steven D'Amico

All rights reserved. Published by Arthur A. Levine Books, an imprint of Scholastic Inc., *Publishers since 1920*.

SCHOLASTIC and the LANTERN LOGO are trademarks and/or registered trademarks of Scholastic Inc.

Library of Congress Cataloging-in-Publication Data

D'Amico, Carmela.

Ella sets the stage / by Carmela D'Amico ; illustrated by Steven D'Amico.– 1st ed.   p. cm.

Summary: Believing that she has no special abilities to share in the school talent show,

Ella the elephant takes over the event's organization and discovers something important in the process.

ISBN 0-439-83152-0

[1. Talent shows–Fiction. 2. Elephants–Fiction. 3. Animals–Fiction. 4. Schools–Fiction.] I. D'Amico, Steven, ill. II. Title.

PZ7.D1837Ela 2006   [E]–dc22   2005022796

10 9 8 7 6 5 4 3 2 1   06 07 08 09 10

First edition, September 2006   Printed in Singapore   46

Book design by Steven D'Amico and David Saylor

The text was set in 20-point Aged.

ello

sets the stage

by carmela & steven d'amico

ARTHUR A. LEVINE BOOKS

An Imprint of Scholastic Inc.

One day toward the end of class, Miss Bell made an announcement.

"In two weeks, our school will be hosting its first talent show."

Ella raised her hand. "What's a talent show?"

"It's a fun and festive event where every student has the chance to get on stage in front of an audience and share their special talent."

For someone as shy as Ella, getting up in front of an audience was as far from "fun and festive" as anything she could imagine.

After school her friend, Tiki, ran up.

"Isn't it exciting?" she asked. "Of course, I'll be putting on a magic show with Lola."

Belinda, who'd been taking ballet lessons for a week, tiptoed up and said, "I can't wait to win the contest! No one else in school is as good at ballet as I am, or as talented, or —"

"As graceful?" laughed Tiki.

"It's only because I'm not wearing my ballet slippers or tutu," she explained.

Tiki asked Ella, "So, what are you going to do?"
"I'm not sure yet," Ella said. "But I'll come up
with something."

As soon as Ella got home, she looked up "talent" in the
dictionary. She wondered, "Do I have a special natural ability?"

"Maybe I'm a talented drummer."
Bang, bang, bang, b-bang! Bang, bang, bang, b-bang!

"Ella!" her mother shouted from the bakery. "What's that racket?"
"Oh, nothing," Ella replied.
Racket isn't a talent, she thought.

Maybe I'm a talented juggler.
Two coconuts up in the air, three coconuts, four!

"Ouch!" Ella yelped, as one heavy coconut bonked her on the head.

Her mother called upstairs, "What's going on up there?"

"Um, nothing!" Ella said. "I'll be right down!"

As she reached for her apron, she sang to herself very softly. *Maybe I'm a talented singer,* she thought. *Maybe I should sing louder.*

So she did. Ella sang as loudly as she could.

Mrs. Sowenso said to Ella's mother, "You know, my little Daisy couldn't carry a tune either, until I sent her to Miss Melody's School of Song and Dance. Now, she'll be singing in the school talent show!"

"So," her mother said later that day. "A talent show."

"Yes. And the problem is, I'm not talented at anything."

"Nonsense," said her mother. "You have numerous talents. You're an expert cupcake-maker. And you're very good at making people happy. And you're –"

"Mom, I don't mean *those* kinds of talents."

"Well, why don't you recite that beautiful poem you wrote for me on Mother's Day?"

Ella shook her head. "All the other kids would laugh."

At school a few days later, Ella saw a poster:

"Oh, hi, Frankie. I'm looking for the talent show committee."

"I'm it," he said. "And boy, am I glad to see you. Everyone else must be practicing their acts."

"How's your puppet show coming along?" she asked.

"It's not," said Frankie. "I've been too busy with all of this."

"Well," said Ella, "I'm sure I can finish up what needs to be done."

Over the next week, Ella painted signs.

She made awards from ribbons of silk and shiny golden medals.

She found out from her schoolmates what they were
doing for the show and,

with the help of Miss Bell, put together
a program.

When she was working, Frankie stopped by.
"What do you think of the new puppets I made?"
"They're gorgeous!" Ella said. "You're so talented,
Frankie."

Tiki and Lola stopped by too. They performed
a part of their act.

"How do you like it?" Tiki asked.

"I love it!" Ella said. "I absolutely love it!"

"What are YOU going to do?" asked Tiki.

Ella just shrugged and sighed.

On the evening of the talent show, Ella arrived early.
She'd baked chocolate cupcakes and made lemonade
to share with her friends.

Belinda pranced over, and she leaped high in the air. When she did, she heard a tear.

"Oh no!" she gasped. "These are my only tights! Now I can't be in the show anymore!"

Belinda started to cry.

"Don't worry," Ella said. "Earlier, I had to patch a hole in one of the curtains. I have a needle and some thread."

"But I'm supposed to go on first," groaned Belinda.

"I'll be quick," Ella said, and she knotted the final stitch in Belinda's tights ...

...just in time for Miss Bell to introduce her.

Ada and Ida, identical twins, performed magnificent jump rope tricks.

Victor played the lovely but challenging "Sunrise Sonata" by Tuskanini.

Frankie put on his puppet show. The audience
stomped and laughed and cheered.

Daisy Sowenso sang the "Elephant Island Anthem."
Her voice was strong and clear. Ella sang along softly.

Tiki and Lola were nearing the grand finale
of their magic act when a loud noise burst from
backstage, startling Lola, who leaped to the rafters.

Theodore's volcano had exploded!

Lola chattered fearfully,
refusing to come down.
Ella thought of how much
Lola loved her hat.
Then she had an idea.

"Come on, Lola! Jump!
You can do it, Lola!"

Lola finally did. The audience cheered and cheered.
Tiki was relieved. She had gotten her grand finale.

The judges had made their decisions.
Miss Bell made the announcements.

"You've all done such a wonderful job. And some of you were outstanding. Frankie, Tiki, Belinda, and Victor: These awards go to you."

A minute or so later, Miss Bell made another announcement.

"The award winners would like to acknowledge a very special friend. Come on out here, Ella!"

But Ella was so shy.
How could she get on stage in front of
an audience who was applauding her?
She didn't think she could.

Then again, she also used to think she had no talent.

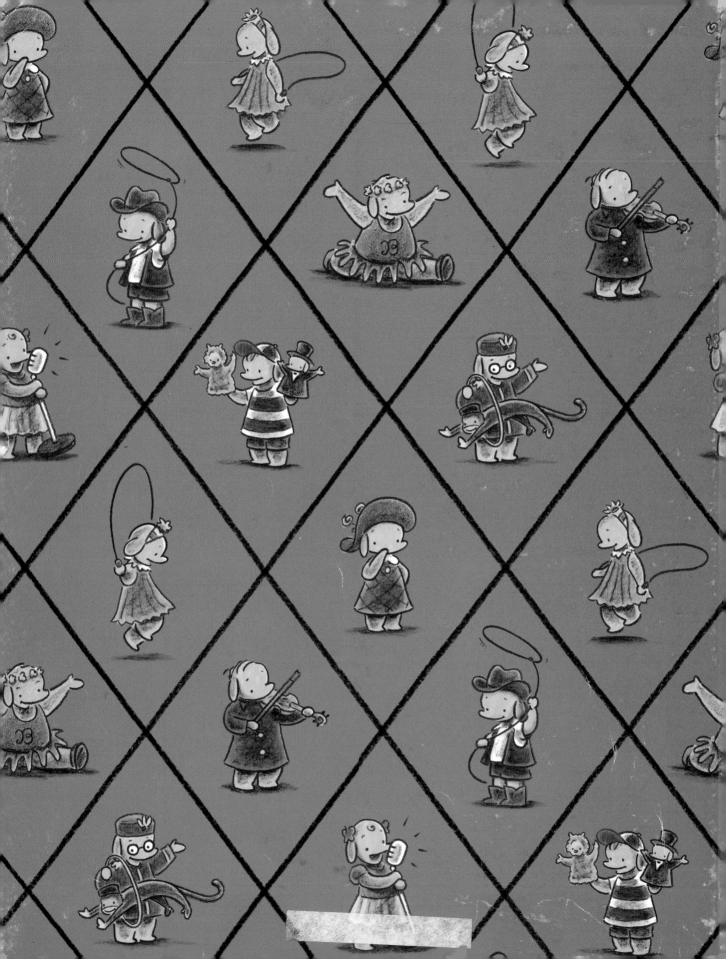